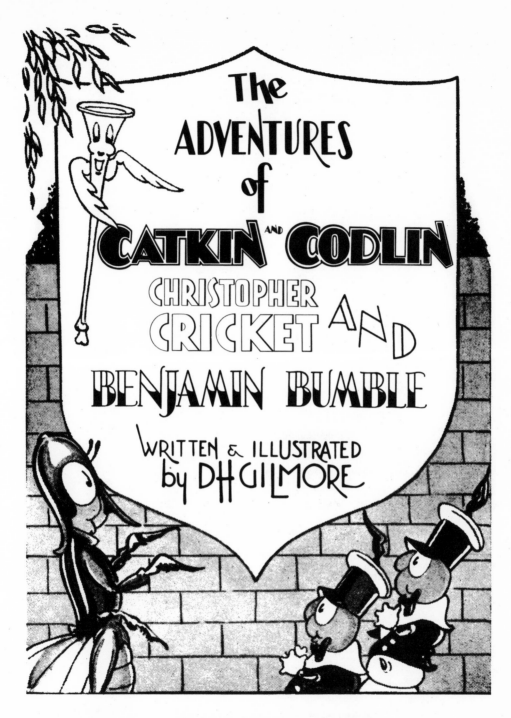

The ADVENTURES of CATKIN and CODLIN CHRISTOPHER CRICKET AND BENJAMIN BUMBLE

WRITTEN & ILLUSTRATED by DH GILMORE

ANGUS & ROBERTSON PUBLISHERS

Angus & Robertson Publishers

London ● Sydney ● Melbourne ● Singapore

Manila

First published in this form by Angus & Robertson Publishers, Australia, 1977

© *D. H. Gilmore 1946, 1946, 1947; This combined edition 1977*

National Library of Australia
card number and ISBN   0   207   13325   5

Printed in Singapore

CATKIN
AND
CODLIN

ONCE upon a time there lived, in the topmost boughs of an old mulberry-tree, two fat little Silkworms. Their names were Catkin and Codlin.

Now, Catkin and Codlin were twins, and so very much alike that even their mummy found it hard to tell which was which. So she made each of them the neatest little jacket and cap–Catkin's was BLUE. and Codlin's a nice, bright RED–then it was easy to tell at a glance who was who!

Mrs Silkworm was a poor widow, and all day long, and sometimes far into the night, she worked at her spinning wheel spinning the finest of fine silk to sell at the Market Town.

One day, Mrs Silkworm set her spinning wheel

whirring and whirring; and by nightfall had spun a large bundle of silken thread of the palest golden hue.

"Indeed it is fit for a king!" said she. "Tomorrow I must take it to the market, for it will be market day and someone will certainly pay a fine price for such beautiful silk."

But, alas! When morning came, poor Mrs Silkworm had a dreadful cold in her head, and could not leave her bed!

"Oh dear! What is to be done?" she sighed. "We

sorely need money; and unless the silk is sold, I fear we will go cold and hungry."

Catkin and Codlin were very sorry to see their mummy so sad.

"Let *us* go to the Market Town," they said.

At first Mrs Silkworm was doubtful.

"It is a long way; and you are very small," she said.

But the Twins pleaded so hard, and the money was so greatly needed, that at last Mrs Silkworm agreed to let them go.

So, with the package of silk carried carefully on a pole between them, Catkin and Codlin set out bravely upon their journey; clambering along the branches in the cool green shelter of the mulberry-leaves.

Presently they came to a place where the leaves ended and there was only the long bare trunk leading to the ground. And just as they reached it there was a *"Chirp!"* and the sound of beating wings as a large bird fluttered on to a branch above them, his bright eyes shining hungrily.

The two tiny Silkworms trembled.

"Quick! Let us hide!" whispered Catkin.

"Where?" Codlin asked.

"In here," Catkin replied, dropping his end of the

pole and diving head first into a hole in the branch.

Codlin followed him; and the silk, which in their fright they had quite forgotten, tumbled quietly off the branch.

The Twins found that the inside of the branch was

quite hollow forming a kind of tunnel sloping down towards the tree-trunk.

"Let us follow this tunnel," said Catkin. "It may lead us to another part of the tree where we can get down to the ground without the bird seeing us."

Very carefully they crawled along inside the branch. At first it was not quite dark for a dim greenish light found its way through many little cracks and crannies in the wrinkled bark; but presently it became very much darker and the floor began to slope very steeply downwards.

"Why, I do believe the whole tree is hollow!" cried Catkin.

"It—it's very dark!" said Codlin nervously. "Do you think we should go on?"

But it was too late to try to turn back, for now the tunnel went straight down like a chimney, and they were slipping and sliding, faster and faster, as they went.

The tunnel ended in a large dim cavern lit by the feeble light of a few glow-worms, and with great straggly

roots twisting about in all directions. Set in the roots was a tiny brown door.

"I wonder who can live down here?" said Catkin. "It must be *very* damp and uncomfortable."

"Let's knock at the door and find out," Codlin suggested.

This seemed a sensible idea; so Catkin, seizing the knocker, gave a hearty "RAT-A-TAT-TAT!!" which wakened astonishing echoes among the roots.

Presently they heard slow, shuffling footsteps on the

other side of the door, followed by the sounds of bolts being drawn very slowly.

At last, with a creak of rusty hinges, the door slowly opened and a quaint little creature in brown overalls with an old-fashioned lantern in his hand peered sleepily out.

"Who are you, and what do you want?" he asked in a drowsy voice. "Don't you know it's only half past September, and I *never* get up before summer?"

"We—we're very sorry to have wakened you," said Catkin politely. "But you see, we were escaping from a Bird, and—"

"A BIRD!" cried Brown Overalls, becoming very wide awake in an instant. "Quick! Quick! Come inside, and shut the door!"

He whisked them through the doorway and started pushing home all the bolts and bars, muttering to himself, "Birds! Dreadful BIRDS! Oh dear, I thought I was safe; but they've even followed me down *here*! Hush! is that the flutter of a wing I hear."

It took Catkin and Codlin a long time to explain that the bird was *outside* the tree; and to tell how they had escaped through the hollow branch and tree-trunk.

"Then why couldn't you say so at once?" said Brown Overalls. "I declare I feel quite limp. I must have a sip of sap to steady my nerves!" Taking a mug from a shelf, he turned a tap set in a root jutting out from the wall.

A stream of crystal-clear sap gushed out and filled the mug. Brown Overalls took a large gulp, and sighed happily. "There's nothing like sap to set you up," he said.

The Twins looked about them and found they were in a large burrow, which Brown Overalls had made very snug and comfortable.

"Do you always live down here?" asked Codlin.

"Yes," replied Brown Overalls. "Once, when I was a tiny child, I lived on a branch of a tree. But I was always a restless child, and one day I tumbled off. Oh dear, I *was* frightened! Dreadful BIRDS were flapping about; so I started to dig, down and down, until I found this safe place where there *aren't* any birds. Of course," he added, "it isn't a palace; but I find it very cosy and convenient."

"Isn't it rather lonely?" Catkin asked.

"Lonely?" cried Brown Overalls. "Oh dear, no! Why, I've the Ants and Mr Mole-Cricket for neigh-

bours; and a Worm or two drop in now and again. Oh, no, it's not *lonely*."

"But don't you long for trees and sunshine?" asked the Twins. "*We* would."

"Sometimes I do," sighed Brown Overalls. "But I must stay down here until I grow bigger and stronger

and less nervous of Birds. Then, one day, when the sunshine is hot and bright above, I'll burrow my way up and out. When that time comes, I'll say good-bye to these old brown overalls for ever."

Just then there was a tap on the door.

"Ah! That will be Mole-Cricket!" cried Brown Overalls jumping up. "He often drops in about this

Set in the roots was a tiny brown door.

"Why, it's Lucy Ladybird!" cried Mr Mole-Cricket. "How ever did you get down there?"

time to give me the latest news of the world up above."

He opened the door, and in stepped a neat little dark gentleman with very bright eyes, long whiskers, and *very* large fore-paws–it was Mr Mole-Cricket.

"Come in! Come in!" welcomed Brown Overalls. "What is the latest news from the big world above? How is Baron Bumblebee behaving?"

"Oh," replied Mr Mole-Cricket, "*he's* up to his old tricks as usual."

"He *is* a wicked creature, to be sure," said Brown Overalls.

"No one worse," agreed Mr Mole-Cricket. "Always robbing and bullying anyone weaker than he is; and hiding away in his Dismal Castle when he thinks he may be punished. It's time someone taught him a lesson."

"I quite agree," nodded Brown Overalls. "And what other news have you to tell me?"

"The creatures living in the tree above us," said Mr Mole-Cricket, "are *very* careless. The way they *drop* things! Why this morning, as I popped out of my burrow for a drop of dew, a great package of *silk* came tumbling down almost on top of me. Gave me quite a turn, I can tell you."

"Oh dear!" cried the Twins. "That was *our* silk!"

"Indeed?" frowned Mr Mole-Cricket. "Then all I can say is that it is a fine state of affairs if a gentleman can't step out of doors without other people throwing silk on his head. I wonder you're not ashamed to admit it."

But when they explained how it happened, he quickly forgave them, adding kindly that if it were a case of "BIRDS", of course everyone quite understood what *that* meant.

"Please, Mr Mole-Cricket," said Catkin, "do you know where the silk is now? We should be taking it to market, and our mummy will be anxious if we're away too long."

"Why, of course," chirped Mr Mole-Cricket. "Just you follow me and I'll show you. Sorry to have to leave you so soon, Brownie, old man; but I think our young friends should be on their way without delay."

They said good-bye to Brown Overalls, and Mr Mole-Cricket led them up a long winding stairway; up and up until they saw sunshine streaming through an opening at the top.

Mr Mole-Cricket peeped out first to make sure there was no danger; and then they stepped out among the moss and tall grasses at the foot of their old mulberry-tree.

"Let me see," remarked their friend, peering here and there. "Where *is* that silk? Humn! Strange! I was sure it was just here when I came downstairs. Now *where* can it have gone?"

They searched here, there and everywhere; but, alas, no silk could they find!

"Oh dear!" sighed Catkin. "Our poor mummy needed the money for that silk!"

"And now we've gone and lost it!" sniffed Codlin.

"Perhaps someone has picked it up," said Mr Mole-Cricket. "Let us walk along the road and see if we can meet anyone who can tell us anything about it."

They set off along the road, peering into hedges and under leaves as they went. But still there was no sign of the package of silk.

At last, as they were passing an old well at the road-side, they heard a pitiful little voice crying, "HELP! HELP!" and the sound of splashing.

Quickly they lowered the wooden bucket down the well, and turned the handle to wind it up again. When it reached the top there was a tiny wet creature clinging tightly to it.

"Why, it's Lucy Ladybird!" cried Mr Mole-Cricket. "How ever did you get down there?"

"I-it was the w-w-wicked B-b-baron B-b-b-bumblebee," sobbed the poor little Ladybird.

"Tell us how it happened," said Mr Mole-Cricket, as they helped Lucy to her cottage which was close at hand.

"I was out for a walk," Lucy told them, "and I found a beautiful parcel of silk near an old tree."

"Our silk!" cried the Twins together.

"I thought it must have fallen

from the tree, and I was going to take it back. But the tree was very high and the silk was very heavy, so I thought I would come home and rest for a little while first. Then, just as I got to the well up rushed that wicked Bumblebee, and seized the silk.

"The villain!" cried Mr Mole-Cricket in a rage.

25

"He said he wanted it for a cosy bed because it was chilly at the Castle," said Lucy. "And when I told him that it wasn't my silk, he cried: 'Stolen, hey?' and pushed me down the w-w-well!"

"That settles it," said Mr Mole-Cricket. "This has gone far too far! Baron Bumblebee is going to be taught a LESSON. He may hide in his Dismal Castle; but we shall follow him there, and teach him GOOD MANNERS!"

With Catkin and Codlin following close behind him, Mr Mole-Cricket marched boldly along until they came to the dark and gloomy wood which surrounded Dismal Castle on all sides.

It wasn't a cheerful place to be sure; and to discourage any visitors, the Baron had placed large notice-

boards all along the path threatening all kinds of dreadful penalties to anyone rash enough to try and follow him to his home.

As they read these notices, Catkin and Codlin began to feel a little nervous; but the angry Mole-Cricket took no heed of the warnings.

"A LESSON!" he kept muttering. "That's what he needs; and that's what he'll get. He'll be the Baron HUMBLEbee when I've done with him!"

He strode along at such a pace that the Twins found it difficult to keep up with him; but as no one appeared to bar the way or turn them back, they began to feel much braver.

Presently they came in sight of a strong, high wall and beyond it the dark towers and turrets of Baron Bumblebee's Dismal Castle rose towards the tree tops.

In the wall was a great, gloomy gateway; but it was shut fast.

In the centre of the gate was a great brass knocker with a notice under it:

"PLEASE RING"
and at the side was a bell-pull with a notice above it:
"PLEASE KNOCK".

This was a Cunning Scheme of the Baron's to baffle visitors and send them away in despair; but it didn't baffle Mr Mole-Cricket at all. He just pounded away at the knocker with all his might while Catkin and Codlin swung on the bell-pull.

The noise was dreadful!

But there was no sign of the gate being opened; so they started pounding and ringing afresh.

"Perhaps the Baron's deaf," Catkin suggested.

But suddenly a small window in a high turret opened, and out poked the ugly head of a very fat Spider.

"Go away!" he ordered. "Stop that dreadful din and GO AWAY!"

"Oh no," replied Mole-Cricket. "We've come to see the Baron on Important Business. Come down and let us in."

"The Baron is very busy and can't be disturbed," growled the fat Spider. "Go away and come back tomorrow, or next day, or the day after that," and he slammed the window shut with a bang.

Then Mr Mole-Cricket began to pound on the gate with a heavy stick.

"I'll see the Baron," he cried, "even if I've got to break his gate down first."

But this wasn't necessary; for at last there was the sound of bolts being drawn and the great gate swung open a little. The ugly face of Spider peered out at them grinning with rage.

"So you won't go away, won't you?" snarled Spider. "Then come in and see what happens to you."

He flung the gate open and they stepped into a damp-looking courtyard.

"Take us to your master the Baron," ordered Mr Mole-Cricket boldly.

"Oh yes indeed," replied Spider, slamming the gate behind them. "You'll be taken to the Baron, never fear."

Suddenly he cried, "Ho, there!" and out of the shadows there sprang a host of horrid little creatures, who seized Catlin, Codlin and Mole-Cricket, and, in less time than it takes to tell, had all three very securely and uncomfortably bound with strong cords.

"Heh! Heh! Heh!" cackled Spider in triumph. "*Now* perhaps we're not feeling quite so clever. Perhaps you'd rather NOT be taken to my master the Baron, eh?"

31

At this all the horrid little creatures laughed very heartily, and the sound was not at all pleasant to hear.

Catkin and Codlin shivered with fear; but the brave Mr Mole-Cricket only said, "You'll be sorry for this, you great *fat* Spider."

Baron Bumblebee sat in his great Baronial Hall counting his treasures. The fact that most of them had been stolen from other, weaker creatures didn't trouble *him*. He was rather proud of being the wickedest Bumblebee in all the world; and, as he patted the large package of shining silk that he had just added to his pile, he hummed a song to himself.

There was a knock at the door, and the ugly head of Spider peered round the edge of it.

"Three visitors for your honour," said Spider.

"Aha! Let's have a look at them," cried the Baron; and three wriggling bundles were pushed roughly into the room.

The Baron peered down at them.

"Well, well!" he exclaimed. "If it isn't old Mole-

Cricket, himself. And you've got two little friends with you, I see. Ha! Ha! The more the merrier—eh, Spider?"

Spider cackled gleefully.

"I hear you've been making threats against me," went on the Baron. "Now that was very rash of you, my good Moley. For I don't like threats; they upset my finest feelings; and I've got ways of punishing foolish creatures who threaten *me*!"

"Oho!" cried Spider. "Threats, eh? That's a serious thing, that is. Worse than trespassing—lots worse. Shall

Baron Bumblebee sat in his great Baronial Hall
counting his treasures.

With a clash and a clang the great door shut, and the key
turned in the heavy lock outside.

I boil 'em in oil, your honour? I can heat a pot in no time."

Catkin and Codlin held their breath and trembled.

"No-o," said the Baron slowly. "I don't think I'll boil them—at least, not yet. I want to think up some very special kind of punishment for this interfering Mole-Cricket, and at the moment I have other pressing matters to attend to."

"You'll regret this, Baron Bumblebee," said Mr Mole-Cricket. "I warn you that your wickedness has gone too far and before very long you will be punished as you deserve.'

But the Baron pretended not to hear.

"Tell me, Spider," said the Baron. "Is the dampest, darkest dungeon empty at the moment?"

"It is," replied Spider.

"Then take them down there. Set a guard outside the door and see that they don't get too much to eat. I'll teach them not to poke their noses into other people's affairs. Take 'em away!"

Down long, dark stairways and gloomy passages the three captives were carried and at last flung into the dampest, darkest dungeon—THUD!—THUD!! —THUD!!!

With a clash and a clang the great door was shut, and the key turned in the heavy lock outside.

Deep down among the tree-roots, a wandering wormlet popped his pointed nose into Brown Overalls's burrow.

"Heard the news?" he asked.

"What news?" asked Brown Overalls rather grumpily. "I haven't seen Mole-Cricket for ages, and *he's* the only one who remembers that I'm interested in what goes on up above."

"Why," cried the Wormlet, "that's just it! Old Moley has disappeared! Hasn't been seen for ages. Lucy Ladybird says he set off for Dismal Castle with two little Silkworms vowing he was going to teach the Baron a lesson, and no one has heard of him since."

"Dear, dear, dear!" exclaimed Brown Overalls.

"This is terrible! Why, Mole-Cricket was my best friend. I must do something to find him."

He paced up and down his burrow in great distress, and kept looking at his rather curious clock—it told the time in years and months instead of hours and minutes; for, you must know, time passes *very* slowly for little folk like Brown Overalls.

"Only quarter to October," he sighed. "That's dreadfully early. Winter can scarcely be over; and the Birds will be hungry and fierce!"

The thought made him shiver. But nothing could be done for his friend Mole-Cricket while he stayed there in his snug and cosy burrow.

"Oh well," he said bravely, "my clock may be

wrong, and it really may be much later. And after all, what do birds matter when old Moley's in trouble?"

And without further delay, Brown Overalls selected  a soft place in his ceiling and began scraping and burrowing among the roots as fast as he could, working his way upwards, ever upwards.

In their damp and dreary dungeon Catkin, Codlin, and Mr Mole-Cricket had lost all idea of time. Their prison was so deep and dark that they couldn't tell daytime from night; and Spider, remembering the Baron's warning, only pushed food through a hole in the door at very long intervals, so counting mealtimes wasn't any help.

"I think the Baron has forgotten us," said Catkin.

"I hope he has," Codlin replied. "*I* don't want to be boiled in oil!"

"Cheer up!" chirped Mr Mole-Cricket, who had never lost heart; perhaps because he was as much at home *under* the ground as above it. "You never know when something may pop up."

And at that very moment something *did* pop up!

There was a scuffling and scraping beneath the floor, and suddenly a brown head and a very dirty face shot up in the very centre of the dungeon.

"BROWN OVERALLS!" cried Mr Mole-Cricket.

"Well!" said Brown Overalls, wiping a dab of mud from his nose, and trying to look stern. "A fine pickle you're in, Moley, I must say. Not to mention our two young friends here who look most uncomfortable."

"You *do* love to scold," chuckled Mr Mole-Cricket. "But I deserve it; for I was careless to walk into the Baron's trap so very easily."

"Just plain foolish I call it," grumbled Brown Overalls, hastening to untie them. "You should have

41

asked *me* for advice, before dashing off like that into danger!"

As the last cords slipped from the captives, the horrid voice of Spider was heard on the other side of the thick dungeon door. He was speaking to the guard in the passage outside.

"Come, wake up, sleepy-head!" he growled. "The Baron has gone away for the day; and, as I'm tired of feeding these useless creatures, I'm going to boil the lot of them. Open the door and lend a hand to carry them out."

"Now is our chance," whispered Mole-Cricket. "Spring on them quickly as they come in. That's Spider's own trick; we'll see how *he* enjoys it!"

Quickly they crouched down in a corner as Spider and the guard entered the dungeon and peered about in the gloom looking for the captives.

"*Now!!*" shouted Mr Mole-Cricket. And before they knew what had happened, Spider and the guard were bowled over with Mole-Cricket, Brown Overalls, Catkin and Codlin all on top of them at once!

The two wicked creatures roared for help; but the Baron was away and had taken all his horrid little creatures with him, and no one came to their aid.

In a very short time they were completely helpless.

"There!" said Mr Mole-Cricket in a satisfied tone. "As neat a job of tying-up as anyone could wish to see."

Everyone agreed, except Spider and the guard, who took a very dim view of it.

"Oh, p-p-pray good, kind, noble gentlemen," blubbered Spider. "D-d-don't hurt me! I am really a very soft-hearted, gentle creature. Wouldn't hurt a f-f-fly, I wouldn't. Let me go, kind sirs, and I'll show you where all the Baron's finest treasures are hidden."

"I suppose," said Brown Overalls sternly, "it was for kindness you tied up my friends, here; and kept them half-starved in this dismal place for long, dreary months?"

"O-o-o-o-h!" whimpered Spider. "These ropes are hurting!"

"They won't be so tight when you've missed a few meals," said Mole-Cricket. "Try whistling when you're hungry, Spider; it's a great comfort, so I've found."

Without heeding the pleadings of Spider or the groans of the guard, Brown Overalls led the way out of the dungeon.

Now, as they climbed upwards, the stairways and passages became warmer, and this seemed to make Brown Overalls strangely excited. He began to hurry, faster and faster, looking back at the others over his shoulder.

"Do hurry, you fellows!" he cried. "How slow you are! Can't you climb faster than that?"

"Whatever *is* the matter with him?" puffed Mr Mole-Cricket to the twins.

"Sunshine!" shouted Brown Overalls suddenly. "That's what it is. I can feel SUNSHINE!"

He scampered up the stairs two at a time, leaving the others far behind. They heard his voice getting fainter in the distance chanting, "SUNSHINE, SUN-SHINE, SUNSHINE."

Puffing and panting, Catkin and Codlin and Mr Mole-Cricket came at last to a door which opened on to a walled courtyard. And there, in the sunniest, warmest corner was their friend, Brown Overalls.

But he seemed changed. His brown overalls were getting tighter and tighter; until suddenly, with a loud "POP!" all his buttons burst at once, and out stepped a handsome Prince in beautiful shining black armour.

The Twins were too amazed by this startling change to say a word; while Mr Mole-Cricket could only stammer, "B-b-brown O-o-overalls!" in a faint voice.

The shining Black Prince bowed to them.

"My good friends," he said, "I am sorry if this sudden change in my appearance has startled you. But perhaps you remember that I *did* tell you that one day I would leave my dark burrow, and have done with my old brown overalls for ever."

"Why, of course we remember," they cried.

"From now on," he continued, "I am Black Prince Cicada. But, though I've changed my clothes and my name, you'll find I'm still plain 'Brown Overalls' when it comes to helping my friends, and keeping an eye on my rash friend Moley, here."

With that he shook hands with them all round.

"Now," said the Black Prince (for we must now call him by his right name), "we mustn't forget our wicked old friend the Baron. You came here to teach the old rogue a lesson, and a lesson he shall have."

"But *how*?" they asked.

For reply, the Prince unfolded a pair of strong and shimmering wings and flew up to the topmost turret of Dismal Castle. While his three friends watched and wondered, he drew forth from somewhere in his shining armour a tiny drum and a pair of drumsticks.

"Just you listen to this," he called down to them; and he began to beat upon the drum:

"Trrr-trrr-trrr-*trrah*-JAH! Trrr-trr-*trrah* JAH! *Trrah*-JAH!"

Louder and louder, until, down from their bushes and up from their burrows, a host of tiny creatures presently gathered to find out what all the noise was about.

"My friends," cried the Black Prince. "You will be glad to hear that the Bad Baron will shortly be a Reformed Character. As yet *he* doesn't know it; but he soon will. Of course as a Reformed Character the Baron will have no further use for the treasures which he has from time to time—ahem!—*borrowed*, and which he has been looking after so carefully in this great strong castle. So, if my good friend Mole-Cricket will kindly open the gates, everyone can just step inside and help himself, and that will save the Baron a lot of trouble."

When the gates were opened there was a great scramble and much happy laughter as treasures were found by their owners who had thought them lost for ever.

In a very short time the Baron's great castle was quite empty.

"Lesson Number One," chuckled the Black Prince. "Always return what you borrow. Won't Bumblebee be surprised?"

But they hadn't finished with the wicked Baron yet.

"Get a spade, Moley," said Black Prince. "And you two Silkworms get buckets," he added to Catkin and Codlin.

"Are we going to the seaside?" asked the Twins in wonder.

But the Black Prince led the way out of the castle.

Through the dark wood he led them among the notices until they came to a sharp bend in the path. "I think this will do," said the Black Prince. "Start digging, Moley."

Mr Mole-Cricket dug and dug and dug until there was a deep pit in the middle of the path. Then Catkin and Codlin set to work with their buckets and filled it to the brim with cold, cold water. Last of all they covered the pit with twigs and earth until it looked just like part of the path.

"Oh, *won't* Bumblebee be surprised!" they chuckled as they hid in the bushes and waited.

Baron Bumblebee certainly *was* surprised.

It was almost dark when he came bumbling along followed by all his horrid little creatures.

There was a "CRRRACK!" and a "SPLOOOSH!" and the Baron found himself in a cold, dark, muddy pit, while his horrid followers were suddenly set upon by

"So if you promise to behave yourself in future
I'll pull you out."

four furious insects armed with stout sticks before whom they quickly fled howling in all directions!

"Good evening, Baron," said Mr Mole-Cricket. "Isn't it a trifle cold for swimming at this time of evening?"

"Oh save me!" gasped the Baron. "I c-c-can't swim."

"Poor Lucy Ladybird couldn't swim," said Mr Mole-Cricket. "Yet you pushed *her* down a well."

"I-it w-w-was o-o-only my f-f-fun!" moaned the Baron.

"Well, now you know how very *funny* it is," said Mr Mole-Cricket sternly "I would leave you to drown, but if I did there would be no one to keep that fat Spider from starving in his dungeon. So if you promise to behave yourself in future I'll pull you out."

"O-o-oh, I'll p-p-promise anything you want," agreed the very unhappy Baron.

So they hauled him out, and it was a very damp and

HUMBLE Bee who stood dripping and shivering on the pathway.

"I don't *think* we'll have any more trouble from *him*," said the Black Prince as they watched the wretched Baron limp sadly off to his dark and deserted castle.

So everyone was happy.

Mr Mole-Cricket took the Twins straight home to their old mulberry-tree where their mummy was waiting for them, completely recovered from her cold, and, of course, very very happy at their safe return.

From the beautiful silk which they had set out to sell, Mrs Silkworm made a splendid waistcoat for Mr Mole-Cricket to show how grateful she was.

Lucy Ladybird soon recovered from her ducking in the well and was none the worse for that unpleasant adventure.

Black Prince Cicada took up his residence in the woods round Dismal Castle where he was soon joined by many other shining Princes in armour of Black, Green, and Yellow; and together they drummed and drummed away all day long in the summer sunshine until the noise of their drumming at last drove Baron Bumblebee from his gloomy castle.

With the fat Spider and all his horrid little creatures he departed for distant parts and none of them were ever heard from again.

ONCE upon a time there was a little brown cricket called Christopher. He lived in a cosy burrow at the foot of an old elm tree on the edge of a large wood.

Now most crickets are cheerful, busy little creatures, shy and modest; but Christopher was just the opposite. He was fat and lazy, grumpy and boastful, and he didn't care a button for anything in the world except food and music. Not other people's music—he didn't think much of that!—but he thought very highly of his own playing.

For Christopher had a long silver pipe of curious design on which he played—with short intervals for meals—all day long and far into the night; and he was quite sure he was the greatest piper in the world.

One evening, as the full moon rose behind the dark trees of the wood, Christopher Cricket hopped from his burrow among the elm roots. Under one arm he carried a roll of music and a twisted music-stand. Beneath the other he held his slender silver pipe.

Setting up the stand on a convenient toadstool, he arranged the music so that it was well lighted by the moonbeams. Then, putting his pipe to his lips, he began to play. Slowly and softly at first, then faster and louder, faster and louder—until it seemed he would blow himself right off the toadstool! Oh, how he played! Trills and runs and quavers chased each other in a whirling tune, until at last he had to pause for breath.

From the foot of the toadstool came a clapping of tiny hands, and out of the shadows stepped little Hoppity Harvestmouse.

"Oh, bravo! bravo!" cried Hoppity. "How beautifully you do play, Christopher!"

"Of course I do," Christopher boastfully replied. "I am the best piper in the world!"

"Are you?" asked the tiny mouse. "My mummy says Piper Pan is, because he can make all living things come

to him when he plays on his pipe. Can you do that, Christopher?"

"I could if I chose," boasted the vain cricket. "But I prefer to keep myself *to* myself. A great piper like me can't mix with everyone, you know. And," he added, "Pan couldn't make *me* go anywhere I didn't feel inclined to go."

"How clever you must be!" Hoppity sighed. "I wish I was!"

"Of course I am," agreed Christopher. "Just you

listen to this—" and putting his pipe to his lips again, he played:

"Tiddley-iddley-iddley-umpty-tumpty-oom-pah!"

He played it very beautifully with lots of expression, and paused at the end  for Hoppity to say how good it was; but before Hoppity could say anything at all, there came from the dark woods the sound of another pipe:

"TIDDLEY-IDDLEY-IDDLEY-UMPTY-TUMPTY-OOM-PAH!"

"What was that?" asked Hoppity nervously.

"Oh, just an echo," Christopher replied, although he didn't feel very sure of it himself.

"Perhaps it's Piper Pan," whispered Hoppity, his big ears pricked up and his whiskers a-twitch as he peered towards the woods. Again came the sound of the strange

pipe, now soft and gentle, like a breeze sighing through tall grasses.

"It *is* Piper Pan!" exclaimed Hoppity. "Listen, can't you hear him calling us?"

Christopher listened, and through the music he heard these words:

"Come all good creatures of fur and of feather,
Come from the meadows and come from the streams,
Come from the wildwood and haste through the
    heather
And list to the Piper—the Piper of Dreams.

"List to my piping that banishes sorrow
Here in the glade where the silver moon beams.
Hasten! Oh haste! For ere sunrise tomorrow
Will vanish the Piper—the Piper of Dreams."

"Extraordinary!" exclaimed Christopher Cricket. "I never heard of anyone playing a pipe and singing at the same time, before. We must look into this, young Hoppity."

But Hoppity Harvestmouse wasn't there!

With nose and whiskers twitching with excitement, he was pushing his way through the bushes in answer to the call of Piper Pan.

Rather sulkily, for he hated having his piping disturbed, Christopher pushed his way through the wood until he came to a glade into which the moon-beams poured in silvery radiance. Seated all round were birds, animals and insects, all listening to a strange figure whose piping filled the air.

He was a queer little man with long pointed ears and nose. Over his shoulder hung a skin cloak and there were flowers in his hair; but his legs were queerly shaped and shaggy and ended in a pair of neat little hooves where most people prefer shoes! Christopher knew at once that Hoppity had been right—*it was the great Piper Pan.*

Pan's fingers fluttered over his pipe, and Christopher found the Piper was speaking to him through the music of the pipe.

"So you *did* come," said Pan. "I rather thought you would, you know.'

Christopher strode forward importantly.

"I came," he said, "to discover who it was dared to interrupt me in the midst of my piping. Do you know, sir, that I am the great Christopher Cricket, the world's greatest and most original piper? Please take your wretched wailing else-where. It spoils my enjoy-ment of my own music!"

"Oho!" piped Pan. "And do you know who I am?"

"Oh yes," replied Christopher rudely. "You're Pan. Some say you're a great piper; but then they've probably never heard me play or they'd know better."

Pan's eyes sparkled with sudden anger.

"Christopher Cricket!" he piped sternly. "For a long time I have watched you getting fatter, lazier, and more conceited day by day. It is time you learned that Pan is master of all living things in field and forest. That is why I called you here tonight on my pipe.'

"I needn't have come if I hadn't felt like it," muttered Christopher. "I just happened to be strolling this way."

"Look at your waistline," Pan went on.

"What's the matter with it?" asked Christopher, glancing down rather nervously. "I think it a very fine waistline."

"Far too fat," Pan replied. "You must have more exercise."

"Wh-what kind of exercise?" asked Christopher.

"Oh, just exercise," came the answer. "Can you touch your toes?"

"Of course I can!" Christopher exclaimed, and putting down his pipe, he tried to show that he could. But he found it much harder than he had expected, and while he grunted and puffed over it, Pan piped three soft notes, and Christopher's pipe extended the neatest pair of silver wings, which Christopher had never seen before.

As Christopher straightened his back, the pipe went fluttering up through the trees.

"My pipe! My pipe!" he cried, jumping into the air after it.

"There, you see," piped Pan, "you're getting exercise already."

But Christopher continued to jump into the air until he could jump no longer. Then he flung himself on the ground and sobbed with rage and disappointment. He did not notice the shadow of a cloud shut out the moonbeams, or hear the

pattering of tiny feet as Pan and the other creatures stole softly away. He lay there and sobbed and sobbed until he fell asleep.

★ ★ ★

Seated all round were birds, animals and insects, all listening
to a strange figure whose piping filled the air.

Christopher found himself plunging head-first into
the dark, cold water of the stream.

He opened his eyes to find the glade lit by the morning sunshine, which sparkled on the dewdrops.

"Dear me!" he said, shaking several dewdrops from his wings. "I must have been walking in my sleep. That would explain the dreadful dream about my beautiful

pipe. Pipes don't grow wings except in dreams. As for Pan—he must have been a dream, too. Exercise, indeed! Pooh for Pan!"

Somewhat stiffly Christopher hopped off to his burrow determined to make quite sure that his precious pipe was safely locked up in its special case.

But alas, when he reached home Christopher Cricket received a horrid surprise. The case lay open wide; but his silver pipe was missing!

He searched everywhere, turning out cupboards and upsetting the furniture in his haste; but not a trace of the missing pipe could he find. At last he was forced to admit that his adventure in the wood was not a dream, and that Piper Pan really had charmed his pipe away. Sinking into a chair he burst into tears.

Suddenly from outside came the notes of a pipe!

Christopher dashed to the door; but as he reached it something fast and furry hit him in the middle of his extensive waistline. There was a grunt and a squeak— Christopher sat down suddenly and stared at Hoppity Harvestmouse who was rubbing a large bump on his head and looking rather dazed by the collision.

"What happened?" asked Hoppity. "Has there been an earthquake?" he added, as he caught sight of the overturned furniture.

"Someone is playing my pipe," cried Christopher. "And I won't have it!"

"Nobody's playing it," said Hoppity. "It's playing itself."

"Nonsense! Pipes can't play themselves!"

"Yours can. I heard it. It's down by the stream and it's playing itself like—like anything!"

"Ah! *I'll* soon teach it to go about playing by itself!" exclaimed Christopher, leading the way out of the burrow. "Just you watch me!"

The pipe was leaning against a willow stump, playing softly to itself, and appeared not to notice them. But the moment Christopher ran forward to seize it, it opened its new wings and shot straight up into the air.

Unfortunately Christopher had not expected this, and, before he could stop himself, found himself plunging head-first into the dark, cold water of the stream; while with a nasty laugh the pipe flew off.

The stream wasn't very deep, but it flowed swiftly, and Christopher was tumbled over a great number of very hard and knobbly pebbles by the current, while poor frightened Hoppity scampered along the bank trying to think of a way to save his stout friend from being drowned.

Fortunately he soon came to a place where a little bank of pebbles ran out into the stream, and running along these the little Harvestmouse just managed to grasp Christopher as he came spluttering and bumping round the bend and to drag him to safety.

At first Christopher could only say: "Ouf-pouf! Glug-gulp!" and make other distressing noises; but presently he began to feel a little better.

"Hush!" he suddenly said. "Look!"—Hoppity looked.

From the reeds on the opposite bank came sounds of splashing and as they looked they caught glimpses of tiny silver wings fluttering.

"What shall we do?" asked Hoppity.

"That's easy," replied Christopher. "Get a large pebble and I'll get one, too. First, you will throw your pebble into the reeds. That will drive it from its hiding place. Then I will throw my pebble with deadly aim and before it can recover I will dash up and capture it. Now then, one-two-*three*!"

Hoppity flung his pebble with all his might. There was a loud "*Squark*!!" and louder splashing and rustling in the reeds.

"It's coming! It's coming!" cried Christopher. "Now, just you watch me, young Hoppity."

But it was not the enchanted pipe that came flapping through the reeds. Instead, it was Gussy Gosling, who had been taking a bath in a quiet pool behind the reeds, and who was very annoyed at being so rudely disturbed.

"Quick!" cried Hoppity. "Run, Christopher, run!"

But Christopher was already running, and before Gussy had crossed the stream, both Cricket and Harvestmouse were scrambling through Christopher's door and slamming it shut tight.

"Oh, dear!" panted Hoppity. "That-*puff*-was a-*puff*-very narrow escape!"

"Let it be a lesson to you Hoppity," Christopher replied. "You should know it's most unwise to throw stones."

"But it was your idea," Hoppity pointed out.

"It doesn't matter whose *idea* it was," Christopher argued. "It was *you* who threw the pebble, and look what nearly happened to *me*!"

He frowned so severely that poor Hoppity felt that somehow it *must* be his fault.

"What shall we do now?" he asked humbly.

Christopher rubbed his head in a puzzled way.

It really was difficult to decide what to do, because, since his ducking, there had been no sign or sound of the enchanted pipe.

"What *I* think . . ." Christopher was beginning when from outside, close at hand, came the sound of piping once more.

Through the door they both rushed and began to search, looking under toadstools and fallen leaves without any success, until a chuckle above their heads caused them to look upwards.

Leaning against the chimney-pot was Christopher's pipe.

"Come down at once!" ordered Christopher, shaking his fists.

"Shan't!" replied the rude pipe. "Hee-hee, you can't catch me!" it warbled, fluttering its wings. "Don't you think it's rather too early for river bathing, Mister Cricket?"

Then Christopher Cricket stopped shaking his fist, and tried to look as if he didn't care a row of toad-stools if the pipe stayed there for ever. Taking Hoppity by the arm he strolled back to the burrow and shut the door tightly after them.

"That was a cunning thing to do," he whispered.

"Was it?" asked Hoppity. "Why? Shall I run and see if I can get a ladder from somewhere?"

"No," Christopher replied. "I have a much more cunning plan than climbing dangerous ladders off which I might easily fall. You must go out and talk to the pipe, making it think it's quite safe where it is; while I will climb cunningly up the chimney from inside and take it by surprise."

Hoppity looked first at his friend's waistline and then at the rather narrow chimney, and wondered. But he thought Christopher must be too clever to get stuck. So outside he trotted, and nodded politely to the pipe, who nodded back in an offhand sort of way, and ran over a few scales.

"Where's the other'un?" it asked.

"Oh you mean Christopher?" Hoppity replied. "I fancy he has lost interest in trying to catch you."

"Well, that's a blessing," said the pipe. "I'm tired of being blown to death by a fat windbag. This is the first holiday I've had in goodness knows how long, and I don't want it spoilt by flying all over the place. I'm a peaceful kind of pipe, I am." He warbled a note or two, then stopped and said thoughtfully, "What *is* that fat Cricket doing? I can hear him sneezing."

"You'd sneeze, too, if you'd been in the stream," Hoppity pointed out.

"Not up the chimney, I wouldn't," the pipe said. "What *is* he up to?"

"Perhaps he's drying himself by the fire."

"Well, he's making funny noises about it. Very funny!" said the pipe.

Hoppity felt anxious. Christopher certainly *was* a long time climbing the chimney. Then —"*A-a-ah-tisss-shooo!!*"—there came a sneeze, so violent that it shook the windows and blew the pipe from its perch on the chimney-pot in a cloud of soot.

84

Quite forgetting the Cunning Scheme, Hoppity dashed back into the burrow. All that could be seen of the stout Cricket were his feet dangling from the mouth of the chimney.

"Oh dear! I feared you'd be too stout for that chimney!" cried Hoppity, tugging at the dangling feet.

"Nonsense!" came the muffled voice of Christopher, between sneezes. "The chimney must have shrunk. Ouch! Don't pull so hard or you'll have me in two pieces!"

With a sudden rush and a bump, down he came in a cloud of soot which got into Hoppity's eyes and nose and set him sneezing and sneezing; while Christopher stamped about in a very *black* rage, kicking the furniture, and leaving soot everywhere.

When they went outside, they found the pipe had flown away again.

"It's not fair!" stormed Christopher. "Piper Pan uses magic, and I haven't any. I'll go to the Witch-o'-the-Woods and ask her for some magic, too!"

Little Hoppity gazed with fear at his friend.

"Oh!" he squeaked in alarm. "You wouldn't dare go near the wicked old W-witch-o'-the-W-woods, would you?"

"I'm not afraid of her," boasted Christopher.

"But she casts wicked spells on animals and insects. Oh, please, Christopher, don't go to the Witch-o'-the-Woods!"

But Christopher was already off, hopping along the track leading to the Wildwoods where, as everyone knew (though few had met her), lived the wicked Witch-o'-the-Woods.

The way turned and twisted between brambles and bracken and the roots of great trees; and the farther he went, the darker and gloomier the Wildwoods got; but Christopher hardly noticed the fact.

The track was plain to follow, and Christopher thought it foolish of people to say it was easy to get lost in the Wildwoods.

"Why, here's a sign-post!" he exclaimed, stopping to look at it. On one arm of the post were the words: "TO THE WITCH'S KIT-CHEN", and on the other, which pointed along the way he had come: "BACK AGAIN".

"Ah," said Christopher Cricket, "I am on the right road. I couldn't get lost if I tried. Oh, I am indeed a clever Cricket, and Pan will be very sorry that he meddled with *my* pipe!" And on he went, heedless of any danger.

Turning a corner, he suddenly came upon an old woman who was gathering sticks, which she piled on a blue-checked apron lying on the ground.

"Good day to you, my good woman," Christopher greeted her. "Can you direct me to the home of the Witch-o'-the-Woods?"

There came a sneeze, so violent that it shook the windows
and blew the pipe from its perch on the chimney-pot.

Christopher sipped it greedily, while the witch watched
him with a strange smile on her lips.

"And what may you be wanting with the Witch-o'-the-Woods?" she asked in return.

Then Christopher told her about his enchanted pipe, and of Pan's unfairness; and how he wanted the Witch-o'-the-Woods to give him some magic more powerful than Pan's so that he could charm his pipe home again.

"Aha!" chuckled the old woman. "If it's magic you want, you've come to the right place for it. Why, this path is a magic one, and yon-der old apron is a magic one, too."

Christopher looked doubtfully at the apron, which certainly did not look a very magical one.

"Perhaps you don't be-lieve me," said the old woman. "Then come and sit beside me, here on these sticks, and see for yourself what a very useful kind of magic apron it is."

Rather cautiously, in case it was some trick, he obeyed, and seated himself beside her on the apron.

Then the old woman chanted these words in a high, squeaky voice:

"Apron of patchwork—of white and of blue—
Show off your paces and what you can do.
Home to our kitchen and strong Witch's Brew!"

To Christopher's astonishment, the apron gave three flaps and sailed through the air like a great bird, with Christopher, the old woman and the bundle of sticks on its back, swooping and diving in and out of the tree-tops in a most alarming manner. Christopher shut his eyes in terror.

Presently there was a gentle bump, and Christopher opened his eyes to find apron and all on the ground before a doorway set in the gnarled roots of a hollow tree, through the cracks and chinks of which steam and smoke hissed and puffed.

"Welcome!" cackled the old woman. "Welcome, O clever cricket, to the poor home of the Witch-o'-the-Woods." Taking a large key from her pocket, she unlocked the door crying: "Come in! Come in, O bold and resourceful cricket. Just step this way."

"Now," said the Witch-o'-the-Woods when they were inside, and she had hung the apron on its peg. "Sit down on yonder stool, my fine piper, and I will prepare some food, for you must be both weary and hungry."

"Ah!" thought the greedy cricket. "This is indeed a kind and sensible old person!" And he sat down on the stool while the witch threw handfuls of this and that into the great pot hanging over the fire and sending out great clouds of savoury steam that made Christopher's mouth water.

When the broth was ready, the witch bade him draw up his chair, and placed a great bowl before him. It tasted even better than it smelt, and Christopher sipped it greedily, while the witch watched him with a strange smile on her lips.

"There's something about this broth," said Christopher between sips. "I don't quite know what—Ho-hum!" he yawned. "Please forgive me, good Witch-o'-the-Woods, but I feel strangely drowsy. Now what was it I came to see you about?—Ho-o-hum!"—he yawned again, and began to nod his head sleepily.

"Heh-heh-heh!" cackled the witch. "Those who sup on witch's brew always sleep sound!"

But Christopher only muttered something about a pipe with goat's legs playing all by itself, and snored gently. Then the witch took a large cage and, opening its door, put the sleeping Christopher inside and snapped it shut again with a large padlock.

"There, my great piper!" she cried. "Sleep while you can. From now on, you will be my song-bird. I'll teach you to whistle and dance to amuse me when I feel dull; and if I get tired of you, I'll use you in one of my spells. Heh-heh-heh!" and she chuckled till she choked.

"But now," she cried, "there's much to be done ere moon-set. I must away at once!" And, seizing her favourite broomstick, she mounted it and sailed out, leaving Christopher snoring in his cage. . . .

"Christopher! Oh please, please waken!"

Christopher opened a sleepy eye slowly. There was little Hoppity, trembling with fear and excitement, shaking the door of the cage with all his might.

"What's the matter? Where am I?" asked Christopher.

"In a cage, in the witch's kitchen," Hoppity told him.

"In a *cage*?" roared Christopher. "Who dared to put the great Christopher Cricket in a cage? Let me out of it!"

"I-I can't," apologized Hoppity. "It's locked, and the witch has taken the key away with her."

"What are *you* doing here?" Christopher asked.

"I thought something dreadful might happen to you, so I followed you through the Wildwoods and hid outside until the old witch went out. I had a dreadful time trying to wake you."

Then Christopher Cricket felt frightened!

He shook the bars of the cage and tried to squeeze through them—but, alas! he was too fat! Pushing and pulling at the door did no good either—the lock was too strong to break. It looked as if Christopher Cricket was very securely trapped.

Then Christopher sat himself down in the cage and sang this VERY DOLEFUL DIRGE:

"Alas! alack! and woe is me!
Oh, hearken to my plaintive cry!
While other creatures roam so free
A miserable captive I!
　　Ah, woe is me!

"Alas! alack! and well-a-day!
Had I not boasted of my skill
And tried to teach Pan how to play
I might have had my freedom still.
　　Ah, well-a-day!

"Alas! alack! Oh fateful stars!
Had I but gone without my dinner
I might have squeezed between these
　　bars
Because I would have been much
　　thinner.
　　Oh, fateful stars!"

It was so touching that Hoppity shed tears of sympathy. But, being a practical little mouse, he soon decided that crying would not help and, looking round for something on which to dry his eyes, he saw the witch's apron on its peg.

"Saved!" he shouted. "The magic apron will carry us home!"

With much pushing and pulling Hoppity at last got the cage with Christopher in it on to the blue-checked apron. Then making his voice sound as much like the Witch-o'-the-Woods' as he could, he chanted:

"Apron of patchwork—of white and of blue
Show off your paces and what you can do.
Take me back home, and friend Christopher, too!"

The apron gave three flaps and sailed away out of the witch's kitchen and high above the tree-tops of the Wild-woods. Onwards they sped, the wind whistling in their ears, until in a very short time the magic apron came to rest gently in the very centre of Christopher's burrow.

How glad Christopher was to see his own familiar home. But, alas! He was still inside the horrid cage.

"I don't suppose you could gnaw through the bars, could you, Hoppity?" he asked anxiously.

Hoppity tried, but the bars were too hard.

"Try breaking the lock with the poker," suggested Christopher.

But the poker slipped just as Christopher put his head through the bars to tell Hoppity how to do things —and *that* was very nearly the end of Christopher Cricket!

At last they had to give it up.

"I do wish I had my pipe," sighed Christopher. "A little soft music would help me to think clearly."

"If only you hadn't been quite so rude to Piper Pan," said Hoppity, "he might have helped us."

"*Might*, indeed!" cried Christopher. "It's the least he could do, since it is all his fault that I am in this sorry plight!"

At that moment there was a knock at the door.

"Don't open it," cried Christopher. "It may be the Witch-o'-the-Woods!"

"No, it isn't," replied Hoppity who had been peeping through the window, "it's Piper Pan!" And, before Christopher could say he was "not at home" to anyone, Hoppity opened the door and in trotted the quaint little Piper of Dreams.

"Well, Christopher," said Pan speaking as usual through his pipe. "You *have* got yourself into a nice pickle."

"You got me into it," stormed Christopher. "If you hadn't enchanted my pipe, I wouldn't have gone to the Witch-o'-the-Woods; and if I hadn't gone there I wouldn't be in this horrible cage."

"And," said Pan, "if a tiny Harvestmouse hadn't been brave and clever enough to follow you through the Wildwoods, you'd most likely be out of your cage and into the witch's cauldron by this time—don't forget that, Christopher Cricket."

He patted little Hoppity, who blushed pink to the tips of his whiskers.

"Now," continued Pan, "I think you wanted a little soft music to help you think clearly. Very well, you shall have it. But think hard, Christopher Cricket, think of all the time you've wasted playing your pipe when others have been busy and industrious; think hard of your boastfulness and laziness and your selfish pride. Be sure you think of those, O Christopher Cricket!"

As Pan piped, Christopher began to think that perhaps he was just a little bit boastful, and a tiny bit lazy, and even just a scrap selfish in an idle sort of way. And once he'd begun to think those things, he found he couldn't think of anything else until he'd decided that if ever he was free again he would try hard to be the most modest, industrious and unselfish creature that ever lived.

He looked up and caught Pan's eye, which was very bright and twinkly and seemed to know everything he had been thinking.

"Now dance!" cried Pan, and his pipe broke into a lovely dancing tune which set Christopher's feet tapping.

Faster and faster went the tune, and faster and faster danced Christopher Cricket until suddenly the piping stopped, and Christopher who had been spinning round the cage like a top, stopped, too, and sat down breath-less.

"There," piped Pan softly. "I think you are a *thinner* as well as a wiser cricket now!"

Seating himself on the magic apron, he piped three notes, and with a flap of blue checks, sailed out of the door and away.

"Oh, Christopher," cried Hoppity. "How slim and hand-some you look now!"

It was true. Gone was the stout waist-line, and now Christopher could step quite easily between the bars of the cage to shake his little friend by the hand and thank him for his courage in rescuing him from the wicked Witch-o'-the-Woods.

"Look!" cried Hoppity. "Here is a parcel addressed to you. Pan must have left it."

Christopher unwrapped the package, and there was

his precious pipe. Its wings had completely vanished; but tied to it was a tiny card on which were these words:

> If you boast when me you play
> You'll find I've wings to fly away.

Trembling with excitement, Christopher raised the pipe to his lips, and, rather timidly at first, started to play:

"TIDDLEY-IDDLEY-IDDLEY-UMPTY-TUMPTY-OOM-PAH!"

And, like an echo, faint and far away, came the sound of that other pipe, played by the greatest piper of all—The Piper of Dreams—

TIDDLEY-IDDLEY-IDDLEY-UMPTY-TUMPTY-OOM-PAH!

BENJAMIN BUMBLE

They came in sight of the beautiful Royal Hive.

THERE were once three Bumblebees who lived under a sunny bank on the edge of a wide meadow. Their names were: Bizz, Buzz, and Benjamin Bumble and they were brothers.

Bizz, the eldest, was rather a bossy kind of bee; always telling the others what to do and how to do it, which took up so much of his time that he had none left to do anything himself.

Buzz was next in age, and *he* liked to talk of all the things he was going to do and how well he would do them when he started—but, somehow, he never *did* get started.

So it was little Benjamin Bumble who got all the work to do in the end; but he was a cheerful little chap and was always far too busy to worry.

Each morning, as the sun rose sparkling on the dew-drops, the three Bumblebees set out to gather wild honey from the meadow flowers.

Bizz would climb to the top of a tall grass-blade to get a good view of the meadow. Then he would call to the others, telling them where the best flowers grew, and explaining just how to gather the honey.

Buzz, seizing the largest honey-jar, would cry: "Just watch me! I shall fill this large jar in no time. Then I expect I shall fill several more. If you'd only watch me you'd soon learn how honey *should* be gathered."

But long before Bizz had climbed his grass-blade or Buzz had finished talking, little Benjamin Bumble would be buzzing busily from blossom to blossom gathering honey into his jar as fast as he could.

So it wasn't really surprising that at the end of the day it was Benjamin Bumble who usually had the heaviest jar of honey to carry home.

Now, one evening the three Bumblebees reached home to find a large envelope in their letter-box. It was addressed: "To: Bizz, Buzz, and Benjamin Bumble, The Meadow"; and was sealed with pink beeswax.

"Who could be writing to us?" wondered Bizz, turning it over and over, and peering at the address.

"What *can* it be about?" cried Buzz. "It looks important."

"Why not open it and find out?" suggested Benjamin Bumble.

"A very sensible idea," agreed Bizz. "Fetch my spectacles, Benjamin Bumble; and Buzz had better light the candle, for it is getting rather dark." When the spectacles were found and the candle lit, Bizz broke the pink seal.

112

Inside was a large pink card:–

Her Majesty The Queen Bee
Invites you to
A PINK TEA at the Royal Hive
on
Princess Honeyflower's Birthday

BRING A BIRTHDAY PRESENT WITH YOU.

Bizz read it out to them.

"Hurrah for Princess Honeyflower!" cried Buzz, excitedly. "I do love birthday parties!"

"It doesn't say a birthday party," Bizz pointed out. "It says a Pink Tea."

"It's the same thing," argued Buzz. "It says it's on the Princess's birthday, and there are sure to be lots of games and special things to eat."

"When do we go?" asked Benjamin Bumble.

They consulted the calendar and found that the very next day was the birthday of the fair Princess.

"We must each take a present," said Bizz.

"Oh, I shall take a very special present," cried Buzz. "It will be the most wonderful present of them all, and the Princess is sure to be delighted with it!"

"What will you take?" asked Benjamin Bumble.

"I haven't made up my mind yet," Buzz replied. "But I'm sure to think of something splendid."

"Let's see how much we have in our money-boxes," said Bizz.

When the money-boxes were opened they found they had just sixpence between them. Bizz had three pennies in his box; Buzz had two pennies in his; and Benjamin Bumble had exactly one penny.

"We can buy our presents tomorrow on our way to the Royal Hive," said Bizz.

Next morning the Bumblebees were up before the first sunbeams, for they had to wash their wings and clean their shoes, and make themselves spick and span for such an Important Event.

Of course Benjamin Bumble was busy; for, while Bizz kept saying that they really *must* hurry or they would be quite certain to be late, and Buzz kept on talking of the really remarkable present he would buy with his two pennies, it was Benjamin Bumble who ironed all the wings and polished all the shoes, besides getting the breakfast and tidying up their little home.

But at last they were ready to start. Bizz locked the door and hid the key under the door-mat, then, with his pennies in a neat little purse, he led the way along the white road which ran beyond the meadow. Buzz followed, jingling his pennies in his hand, while Benjamin Bumble put *his* penny inside his hat for safety and trotted cheerfully along behind.

Presently they came upon a queer little bent old woman in a very ragged cloak.

"Oh, kind sir!" she called to Bizz as he came by. "Pray spare a penny for a tired and hungry old woman!"

"Don't bother me!" replied Bizz rudely. "I have no pennies to spare nor time either. I'm on my way to attend a Most Important Function at the Royal Hive. Stand out of my way or I may be late!" And he hurried on.

When Buzz came along, the poor old woman cried: "Oh, sir! I am tired and hungry. Could you spare just one penny to help me on my way?"

"*One* penny?" cried Buzz. "My good woman, I would gladly give you a *bag* of pennies —if only I had them! But, alas! as you can see I have only *two* pennies.

"With these," continued Buzz, "I am on my way to buy the most wonderful present for Princess Honeyflower. Now, if you happen to be here next week or the week after, I will certainly see if I can't do something to help you." And, raising his hat politely, he trotted after Bizz.

Then along came Benjamin Bumble, and as soon as he caught sight of the bent old woman he felt very sorry for her and wondered what he could do to help her. She looked so very tired and hungry.

So he took off his hat, and, taking his penny out of it, handed the penny to her.

"Here, poor old woman," he said kindly. "I was going to buy a present for the Princess with it; but I expect she will have lots and lots of presents, and you look as if you need a penny more than a Princess does."

"Bless you for your kind heart!" she cried. "And here is a present for you in return."

From under her ragged cloak the little old woman took a dull greyish-blue pebble and gave it to Benjamin Bumble. It certainly was rather an odd kind of present to give; but Benjamin Bumble thanked her politely, and tucked it inside his hat where his penny had been.

"Take good care of it," said the old woman. "For it is indeed an unusual pebble given to my great-great-grandmother by a very powerful fairy. Whoever has the pebble will always be protected in time of danger and find a friend in time of need."

Benjamin Bumble said "Thank you" again, and then trotted off after Bizz and Buzz who were almost out of sight in the distance. He had to trot quite quickly to overtake them.

"Goodness me, Benjamin Bumble!" cried Bizz. "I do wish you wouldn't dawdle so! You'll make us late for the Pink Tea."

"I only stopped to give that poor old woman a penny," explained Benjamin Bumble.

"You did *what*?" cried Bizz and Buzz together.

Benjamin Bumble told them again, and showed them the pebble which the old woman had given him.

"I never heard such foolishness!" Bizz scolded. "Now how will you get a present for the Princess?"

"I could give her my pebble," suggested Benjamin Bumble.

But Bizz and Buzz laughed nastily. "Give a dingy little pebble to a Royal Princess as a Birthday Present?" they sneered. "What an idea!"

"*I*," said Buzz, "am going to buy a Very Special Present, and it is going to cost exactly two-pence."

"And I will need all three of *my* pennies for my present," Bizz added. "So you needn't think you can borrow any of our pennies, so there!"

At that moment, from behind a tree, out sprang three Desperate Characters, all heavily armed.

"Stand!" cried the first, pointing a pistol at Bizz.

"Stand and deliver!" growled the second, waving a club.

"Your money or your lives!" squeaked the third, who was armed with a sharp dagger.

The three Bumblebees were too astonished to move. They just stood and stared.

"Come, come!" shouted the first Desperate Character to Bizz. "Hand over that fat purse and be quick about it!"

Trembling very much, Bizz handed over the purse with his three pennies in it.

"Now you!" said the rogue with the club to Buzz. "How much have you got? Only two-pence? Well, it's better than nothing, so hand it over if you don't want this club to crack your crown!"

For once, poor Buzz had nothing to say, and meekly handed over his two pennies.

"Aha!" squeaked the third villain, poking his dagger at Benjamin Bumble. "*This* one must have *lots* of money!"

"Indeed I have none," replied Benjamin Bumble. "But I will give you this beautiful pebble if your friends will hand back those pennies they have just taken from Bizz and Buzz."

At this the Desperate Characters flew into a great rage and were just about to set upon Benjamin Bumble with all their weapons, when rattling round a corner on a bicycle came a stout blue Policeman, at the sight of whom the three Desperate Characters took to their heels.

Rattling round a corner on a bicycle came a stout blue Policeman.

They hurried faster now in order not to be late for the Pink Tea.

With a loud shout the Policeman gave chase; but he was very stout and his bicycle was very old, and before he had gone far one wheel came off tossing him into a ditch. By the time he had clambered out again the three Rogues had vanished.

So the Policeman limped sadly back to his Police Station to Put In A Report, while Bizz sat down at the roadside shedding tears of rage, and Buzz sat beside him talking about the things he would do if ever he met those Robbers again.

But Benjamin Bumble looked at his pebble and wondered whether it *could* have had anything to do with the timely arrival of the stout blue Policeman to protect him when he was in danger.

Presently they heard footsteps, and round a bend came a very small Caterpillar carrying a very large bundle on his back. He walked very very slowly as if he was dreadfully tired.

"Good day to you, good Bumblebees," he puffed. "I wonder if one of you would help me carry this heavy bundle to my home on the other side of yonder field?"

"Certainly not!" sniffed Bizz. "I have just suffered a Severe Loss, and my nerves are in a dreadful state. Carry your own bundle, do; and don't bother me about it!"

Buzz said: "Carry your load for you? My dear fellow there is nothing would give me greater pleasure. But just now I'm deciding what will be the best punishment for those wicked Robbers, and I simply can't spare any time. Now, perhaps tomorrow——"

But little Benjamin Bumble cried: "I'll help you! Give me the bundle. You look tired out—just lead the way."

The Caterpillar said "Thank you", and led the way.

129

The bundle was even heavier than it had looked, and Benjamin Bumble was very glad when at last they reached the Caterpillar's home on the other side of the wide field. Gladly he set his burden down on the door-step.

"Oh, thank you kind Bumblebee!" cried the Caterpillar, taking out his purse, which had exactly five pennies in it. "Here are five pennies as a reward for your kindness."

Benjamin Bumble was so excited he could hardly say: "Thank you!" before he hastened away to tell Bizz and Buzz of this piece of good fortune.

The fairy pebble, he thought, had certainly brought them a friend when he was indeed greatly needed. *Five* whole pennies! He'd never had so much money! He buzzed happily, thinking of the fine present it would buy.

Bizz and Buzz were still sitting gloomily at the roadside as Benjamin Bumble came buzzing back.

"We've been waiting for you," grumbled Bizz. "We may as well all go home. With no money to buy presents, we can't go to the Princess's Pink Tea."

"Oh yes, we can!" cried Benjamin Bumble. "We have five pennies!" And he told them about the Caterpillar's gift.

Bizz and Buzz pounced on the pennies at once.

"Why it's exactly the number that those Rogues stole!" Bizz said. "Three for me, and two for Buzz."

"But what about *my* penny?" asked Benjamin Bumble.

"Oh, you didn't have a penny," Bizz replied. "*You* only had a silly little pebble." And he hurried along the road before Benjamin Bumble could think of an answer.

Over the next hill they came to a neat village with several shops filled with tempting things to buy. The Bumblebees found it difficult to decide which, of so many fine things, would make the best present.

Bizz bought a large green balloon which cost one penny. Then he happened to see a very fine coat which he thought would make him look a Very Important Person. So he spent the other two pennies on that.

Buzz, after asking the price of everything in the shop and giving the shop-keeper a lot of trouble, at last decided to buy two pink sugar mice. He was very fond of sugar mice himself, and thought that if the Princess didn't happen to like them, they wouldn't be wasted.

As Benjamin Bumble had no pennies to spend, he could only look longingly in the shop windows and think what he would buy if pebbles were only pennies.

At last Bizz and Buzz finished shopping and set out once more for the Royal Hive.

They hurried faster now in order not to be late for the Pink Tea. The sun was high and the road hot and dusty. But Bizz was so proud of his new coat that he would not take it off to get cool, while Buzz kept taking his sugar mice out of their wrapping so often to admire them that they soon became sticky and dusty. Benjamin Bumble trotted along after his brothers, wondering if he would be able to explain to the Princess how he came to have a pebble instead of a present.

At last they came in sight of the beautiful Royal Hive set high on a white platform among the lovely flowers of a large garden, its white walls glistening in the bright sunshine.

A stream of Bees and Insects were climbing the broad stairway to the great door guarded by soldiers with long lances. At the entrance stood a stout old Drone, who kept saying: "Show your presents, please! Only those with presents may come in. Walk up, please, and show your presents." As each one showed his present, the Drone waved him on through the doorway.

Bizz swaggered up in his fine coat and flourished the green balloon before the Drone.

"I am Bizz the Bumblebee," he said. "I have brought this beautiful balloon for the Princess."

The Drone bowed politely to Bizz and waved him towards the great door. Then he turned to Buzz. "Your present?" he asked.

"Present?" cried Buzz. "Do I look as if I would only bring *one* present? No, no! *I* am not a Bee like that! I have *two* presents." He showed two rather sticky pink objects.

"What *are* they?" asked the Drone suspiciously.

"Why, pink sugar mice, of course," Buzz replied.

"H'm!" said the Drone. "They don't look very mouse-like to me; but I suppose they count as a present, so in you go."

Buzz hurried through the great door into the Hive.

Benjamin Bumble began to feel a trifle nervous as the Drone looked in his direction.

"Now, young man," he said, "let me see what you have brought for our beautiful Princess."

Timidly Benjamin Bumble held out the little, dull pebble.

The Drone peered at it, then he peered hard at Benjamin Bumble and frowned alarmingly.

"What *is* this?" he asked. "A joke?"

"Oh no, sir," said Benjamin Bumble. "It's a pebble."

The Drone turned quite purple with rage, and his eyes bulged dreadfully.

"How–how *DARE* you, sir?" he shouted. "I suppose you've spent all your pennies on yourself. And now you've the impudence to bring a dirty little *pebble* and say it's a present!"

"It–it's a Very Special Pebble," said Benjamin Bumble.

But the Drone wouldn't listen. Seizing the pebble from him, he flung it away with all his might into the wide garden.

"Oh dear!" wailed Benjamin Bumble. "You've thrown away my Fairy Pebble!"

"Very sad," sneered the Drone, beckoning to two guards. "Take this Impudent Rascal and throw him after his precious pebble," he ordered.

In a twinkling poor Benjamin Bumble was seized and carried to the edge of the platform. It was high above the ground; but the soldiers just said: "One! Two!! Three!!!"—and over the edge went Benjamin Bumble, to land with a THUD on the hard and knobbly pathway below.

While he was wondering if he was still all in one piece, and feeling rather doubtful about it, along the pathway on which he was sitting came the stout blue Policeman who had put the three Desperate Characters to flight.

In one hand he held his helmet which had a large dent in it, and in the other was the pebble which the Drone had thrown away a few moments ago.

"An Outrage!" he was muttering fiercely. "Knocking the helmet off an officer's head is an Outrage; which besides it's against the Law!" Catching sight of Benjamin Bumble, he scowled fiercely. "Do you know anything about this pebble?" he demanded.

"Why yes," replied Benjamin Bumble. "It's my pebble!"

"Ah!" growled the Policeman. "You just come with me."

It was useless for Benjamin Bumble to try to explain that he had not thrown the pebble. Policeman would listen not to him; but, grasping him firmly, marched him up the stairs to the Royal Hive once more. All the guests had already gone in, and only the soldiers still stood guarding the great doorway.

"Where is Sir Drowsy Drone?" asked the Policeman. "I want him to Make an Example of this Very Dangerous Vagabond who's been a-throwing of pebbles at my new helmet."

"Better take him inside," one of the soldiers suggested.

So inside they went, and found themselves in a large hall with walls of golden honeycomb where many Bees were bustling about; but there was no sign of Sir Drowsy.

The Policeman put down his damaged helmet and the pebble on a small table, and said sternly: "Now you stay here, my lad, while I look for Sir Drowsy Drone. And don't you go for to try to escape, or it will be All the Worse for You!"

No sooner was the Policeman gone than Benjamin Bumble slipped across to the table and picked up his precious pebble. With it in his hand he felt much bolder. On tip-toe he crossed the hall to a door which opened on to the loveliest of gardens.

Just at that moment, a little voice at his side said: "Hello, Bumblebee. You're rather late, aren't you?"

He jumped and looked round. Beside him stood a little Brown Bee—the prettiest, daintiest little creature he had ever seen. He could only stare at her.

"Come on," said little Brown Bee. "I'll show you the way. Have you got your present ready?"

"Oh dear!" sighed Benjamin Bumble. "I haven't one."

"Then how ever did you get in?" asked Brown Bee.

So Benjamin Bumble told her all that had happened to him that day. Brown Bee was very sorry for him. She said it was "A Shame!" and that she would tell the Princess about it.

"Hello, Bumblebee. You're rather late, aren't you?"

Out from the Royal Hive came Her Majesty the Queen Bee.

"I've never been asked to a Pink Tea before and I did so want to see what they were like," said Benjamin Bumble.

"Then you *shall* see it," replied Brown Bee.

"But the Policeman or Sir Drowsy Drone will be sure to see me," Benjamin Bumble pointed out.

"Oh no, they won't," Brown Bee assured him. "I know a place where they will never think of looking. Just you come with me."

Taking him by the hand she led him through the doorway into the lovely garden. No one was about, but from beyond a hedge a great buzzing was going on where the guests were awaiting the arrival of Princess Honeyflower.

Keeping well hidden by the hedge, and closely followed by Benjamin Bumble, Brown Bee hastened through the garden until they came to an old tree growing close beside a brick wall. Its branches were covered with beautiful pink blossoms.

"There you are!" whispered Brown Bee. "Climb up and hide among the blossoms, and you'll be able to see everything. Take care you don't fall down, though. That wouldn't do!"

She waved her hand and sped back to the others, while Benjamin Bumble climbed up among the pink blossoms.

He found himself looking down into the special part of the Royal Gardens reserved for Pink Teas. On all sides were pink flowers—pink roses, pink sweet-peas, pink carnations nodded in the gentle breeze, while pink Canterbury bells chimed softly. Just beneath his tree a dainty bower of pink rosebuds had been made, and on the smooth lawn before it he could see the crowd of guests awaiting the arrival of the fair Princess Honey-flower.

146

Presently, amid loud cheering, out from the Royal Hive came the Princess, carried in a rosy chair decorated with flowers. She smiled and waved to the guests as she was carried to the bower beneath Benjamin Bumble's tree.

Then each guest came up and wished the Princess "Many happy returns", and gave her a birthday present. The Princess thanked each one very sweetly.

Of course, being a Princess, she was very beautiful; but Benjamin Bumble felt sure Brown Bee was even nicer.

Just as Bizz and Buzz came up to the Princess, there was a sudden startling interruption.

A voice cried: "*STAND!*"

Another voice growled: "*Stand and Deliver!*"

While a third voice squeaked: "*Money or your Life!*"

And there, on the garden wall stood the Three Desperate Characters, with pistol, club, and dagger.

"Aha!" said the leader in a nasty tone. "If anybody wants to be shot, clubbed or daggered, he's only to say so. Only too pleased to oblige. But if you're wise you'll let us take those very fine presents without any fuss. After we have finished, you can go on with your party as if we'd never called–unless anyone wants to be shot, clubbed or——!"

But before the Dreadful Threat was ended, a *little, greyish-blue pebble* suddenly whizzed through the air from the branches of the old tree against the wall. It hit one Desperate Character in the exact middle of his waistcoat. With a howl he dropped his pistol and clutched wildly at his wicked companions, trying to keep his balance. But it was no good. Off the wall they all came tumbling in an untidy heap.

But, alas! The effort of hurling his pebble had caused Benjamin Bumble to lose *his* balance. He clutched wildly at the petals of the blossoms to save himself, but they came away in his hands, and next instant he crashed down right in the middle of the birthday presents.

At that moment into the garden rushed the Policeman followed by Sir Drowsy Drone and several Soldiers.

"There he is!" cried the Policeman, pointing at Benjamin Bumble. "That's the Rogue who spoiled my helmet!"

"And who are these?" asked Sir Drowsy, pointing to the Desperate Characters.

The Policeman stared, rubbed his eyes, and stared again in great astonishment.

"Why, your honour," he said; "they looks very much like Henry Hornet, Monty Mantis and Slyme the Slug. Very Desperate Characters they are, and Wanted By the Police."

"Well, the Police can have them. *I* don't want them. They make the garden look untidy," said the Drone. "Take 'em away!"

"Certainly, your honour," agreed the Policeman. "But what about my helmet, and the Rascal who dented it?"

"Take him away, too," the Drone growled. "People who throw stones must be thrown into prison!"

The Policeman pounced upon poor Benjamin Bumble; but just as he grasped him there was a flourish of trumpets, and out from the Royal Hive came Her Majesty the Queen Bee. The soldiers sprang to attention, the Policeman saluted, and Sir Drowsy Drone and the guests all bowed respectfully.

"What is happening here?" asked the Queen looking about the Pink Garden. "Why is the Pink Tea not progressing, Sir Drowsy?"

"Your Majesty!" replied the Drone, bowing low. "The festivities were rudely interrupted by these four Vagabonds; but I assure your Majesty that I have the Situation In Hand. They shall be Instantly Removed."

"What are they accused of?" the Queen asked.

"These three," replied the Policeman, "are Wanted by the Police for Highway Robbery, your Majesty. And this one," he pushed Benjamin Bumble forward, "for throwing stones at my helmet and a-damaging of same!"

"But, your Majesty, he *didn't* do it!" cried a voice.

"Who said that?" cried Sir Drowsy.

"*I* did," said Brown Bee stepping forward. "And it's true."

Sir Drowsy frowned, the Policeman scowled; but little Brown Bee took no notice of them. Instead, she curtsied low to the Queen Bee and told her all about Benjamin Bumble and how he had come to be hidden in the old tree. "And, you see, your Majesty," she ended; "if he hadn't been there, and hadn't thrown his pebble at Henry Hornet, we would all have been robbed."

Then the Queen thanked Benjamin Bumble and said he was a brave as well as a generous Bumblebee.

"You shall be rewarded," said she. "What would you like most?"

"If you please, your Majesty," he replied. "Could I have my pebble?"

The Queen laughed and said that of course he could have it, and that he must stay for the Pink Tea. "And Brown Bee will take special care of you," she added.

"Oh, that will be lovely!" exclaimed Benjamin Bumble.

"Excuse me, your Majesty," the Policeman said. "But what's going to be done about my best helmet that's been a-ruined of by a pebble?"

"Sir Drowsy must buy you a new one," commanded the Queen, "as a punishment for losing his temper."

So when Henry Hornet and his wicked companions had been taken away, the Pink Tea began in earnest with lots of things to eat, and lovely games among the flowers. Brown Bee and Benjamin Bumble had a wonderful time.

And from that day onwards Bizz and Buzz were always most respectful to Benjamin Bumble, never bossing or boasting, and always asking his opinion about things. "For," said they, "we have a brave and generous Bumblebee for our brother! Even the Queen Bee says so!"

THE END

The Story of David Hunter Gilmore

D. H. GILMORE wrote and illustrated his first children's book, *Cuthbert the Caterpillar*, in 1928. After the book was completed, Gilmore relates, Cuthbert became the most travelled insect in the world as he was rejected by publisher after publisher until he finally got into print in 1941. Following the great success of this book there came a string of successors, including the three that have been selected and combined for this volume.

Gilmore is a New Zealander who has spent most of his life dreaming of becoming a writer of books and experiencing the leisurely pace of life he saw being enjoyed by the literary figures he admired in his youth. Looking back at the grand age of seventy he writes, "The fact that during the ensuing 40 years or so I never achieved the environmental freedom to which my youthful ambition aspired is just one of the things I've learned to live with. A Depression and a Second World War, two marriages and the upbringing of two daughters have since conspired to cut such *dreams* down to size. But the satisfaction I have had in my work, and the many friends it has brought me, have more than made up for those things I may have missed . . . Now at the age of three score years and ten I look back upon a mis-spent youth (who doesn't?), a rewarding middle age, and a placid autumn of congenial mediocrity; but what well might be a "winter of discontent" is made warm by a reflected glow of satisfaction in having even fleetingly achieved a youthful dream. I wanted to be a writer; I was a writer; I am content."

For most of his life, writing was something he did after work as he spent his day-light hours first as a cub-reporter, later as a copywriter and lay-out man in an advertising agency, then as a desk bound corporal during World War II and finally back to a newspaper office as country sub-editor.

The most idyllic time in his life was a period of several years after World War II when he was able to devote himself full-time to his writing and drawing in the beautiful environment of post-war Tasmania. It was then that he produced what he believes to be his best work, including *Christopher Cricket* and *Benjamin Bumble*. *Catkin and Codlin* was written a little earlier and published in 1946.

Because of the many enquiries they have received concerning the rather unique work of D. H. Gilmore, Angus and Robertson believed it was time to re-publish this volume as part of its Australian Children's Classics collection.